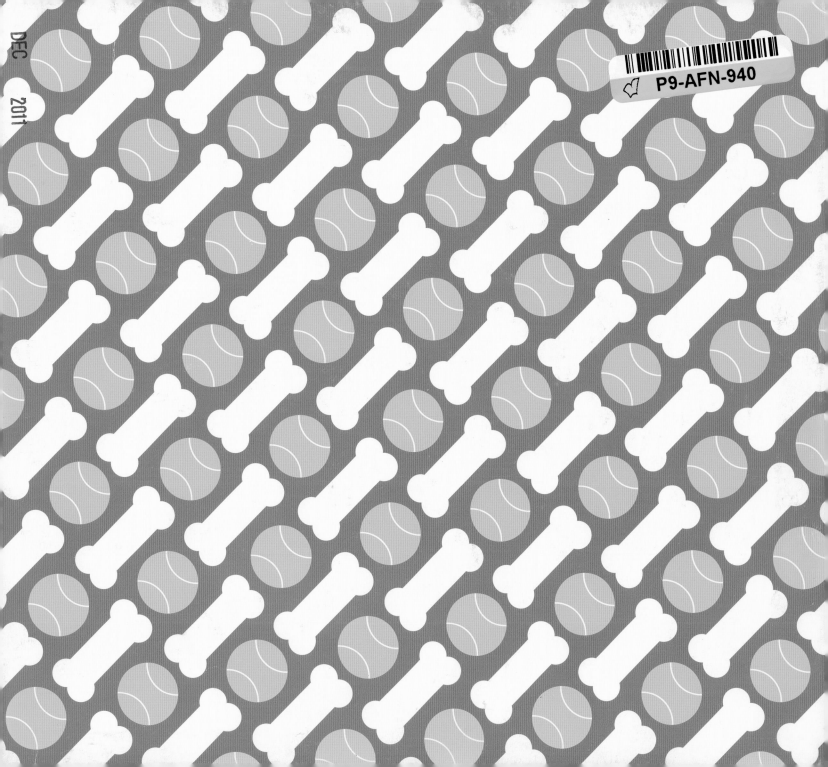

Cataloging-in-Publication Data has been applied for
and may be obtained from the Library of Congress.
ISBN 978-0-8109-8964-1

Book design by Maria T. Middleton

Printed and bound in China
10  9  8  7  6  5  4  3  2  1

Abrams Books for Young Readers are available at special
discounts when purchased in quantity for premiums and
promotions as well as fundraising or educational use.
Special editions can also be created to specification.
For details, contact specialmarkets@abramsbooks.com
or contact the address below.

**ABRAMS**
THE ART OF BOOKS SINCE 1949
115 West 18th Street
New York, NY 10011
www.abramsbooks.com

Dedicated to my muses
**Parker, Kiki, and Eli** (of course)

# Eli, no!

Words & Pictures by Katie Kirk

Abrams Books for Young Readers
New York

# Eli is a good dog,

BEST
DOG

1ST

Winner

FIRST!

Obedience 🐕 School

REPORT CARD

F-

WANTED

★

K9 | ★★★★★★★ ANSWERS TO ELI

BadDogTrainers
Bad to the bone!

21615

21615

CALL: BAD-DOGS

but sometimes bad.

When he eats too much?

When he chases a squirrel?

# Eli, no!

When he makes a mess?

Eli, no!

When he goes where he shouldn't?

# Eli, no!

KEEP
OFF THE
GRASS

When he hogs the bed?

# Eli, no!

When he makes a fuss?

# Eli,
# no!

But...
Though he may whine
and take up the

**bed**

Chase squirrels, dig holes,
and plead

**underfed**

The End.